20,000
LEAGUES UNDER THE SEA

W9-DDJ-863

BY JULES VERNE

Adapted by Judith Conaway

Illustrated by Gino D'Achille

HAMPTON-BROWN

DISCARD

20,000 Leagues Under the Sea by Jules Verne, adapted by Judith Conaway, illustrated by Gino D'Achille. Text copyright © 1983 by Random House, Inc. Illustrations copyright © 1983 by Gino D'Achille. Cover illustration copyright © 1994 by José Miralles. Published by arrangement with Random House Children's Books, a division of Random House, Inc. New York, New York, U.S.A. All rights reserved.

On-Page Coach™ (introductions, questions, on-page glossaries), The Exchange, back cover summary © Hampton-Brown.

Hampton-Brown
P.O. Box 223220
Carmel, California 93922
800-333-3510
www.hampton-brown.com

Printed in the United States of America

ISBN-13: 978-0-7362-2806-0
ISBN-10: 0-7362-2806-3

06 07 08 09 10 11 12 13 14 10 9 8 7 6 5 4 3 2

Many sailors have seen a great monster in the ocean.
A famous professor plans to chase the Thing.

Chapter 1

The stories began in 1866. First they **spread among** sailors. The sailors were scared. Next the people along the coasts **took up** the tales. All over the world, captains and ship owners were worried.

There was a big Thing living in the ocean! A number of ships had seen it. The Thing was shaped like a fish. It was over three hundred feet long. That made it bigger than any known whale!

One ship had seen the Thing blowing **huge jets** of water into the air. Another ship had seen it shining in the dark. Still another ship reported that it had a long spear for a nose. All the ships said that the Thing moved very fast. Faster than any sea animal they had ever seen.

....

spread among were told by
took up started telling
huge jets large amounts

The Americans were the first to act. They brought the ship *Abraham Lincoln* to New York. There it was **armed** to fight a sea monster. Its captain was Commander Farragut.

I myself was in New York at the time. I had been out in Nebraska on a science trip. Now I was on my way back home to France.

My name is Professor Pierre Aronnax. I teach at the Paris Museum of Natural History. I am also the author of a book called *The Mysteries of the Ocean*. Of course, everyone in New York wanted to know what I thought about the Thing.

I believed that the Thing was a giant **sea unicorn**. My idea **settled** the question in most people's minds.

On July 2 a new report came in. A ship had seen the sea unicorn in the Pacific Ocean. Commander Farragut had only twenty-four hours to get ready.

The very next morning I got a letter. It was from the Secretary of the United States Navy. The letter

---

armed filled with weapons
sea unicorn type of whale
settled answered

asked me to sail with Commander Farragut on the *Abraham Lincoln*.

I called my servant and told him to pack our bags. Only minutes before, I had been dreaming about being back in Paris. But now nothing mattered to me except the sea unicorn. I had to be **in on** the chase!

....

in on part of

BEFORE YOU MOVE ON...

1. **Conclusions** Why were the sailors scared of the Thing?

2. **Inference** Reread page 4. Why did people want to know Professor Aronnax's opinion about the sea monster?

LOOK AHEAD Read pages 7–12 to learn about the search for the Thing.

Months pass, and no one sees the sea monster.
Finally, it appears.

Chapter 2

Four months had passed. It was now November 5.
I stood on the deck of the *Abraham Lincoln* and
looked out at the Pacific Ocean. We were about
two hundred miles from Japan. The sky was just
starting to grow dark.

Beside me stood Conseil, my servant. What a
good fellow! For ten years Conseil had followed me
wherever **science led**. He never complained. No
matter what I asked of him, he would answer, "**Just
as Monsieur wishes.**"

Conseil was a happy man. Most of the time he
did not worry about anything at all. But tonight
even Conseil seemed **on edge**. It was our last
chance to spot the sea unicorn. The next day we

....

science led I wanted to go to study science
Just as Monsieur wishes. I will do whatever you want.
on edge nervous

would return to New York. Commander Farragut had given up.

How sad we all were! And how different we had felt only four months before!

Back then, each man on the ship had thought of himself as a **knight in shining armor**. We were out to **rid the world of** an evil giant.

Only two men on board had not been caught up in the excitement. One was Conseil. He never got excited about anything. The other was Ned Land.

Ned Land was a harpooner. He hunted whales with a long spear called a harpoon. He was a great big man. **His eye was quick and his arm was strong.**

Ned's face had a strange, angry look. But he was always friendly to me. Perhaps it was because we both spoke French. Ned was a French Canadian from Quebec.

Ned Land didn't get excited about the monster because he didn't believe in it. Now it looked as if Ned had been right.

"What a waste of time this has been!" I said

....

knight in shining armor hero

rid the world of kill

His eye was quick and his arm was strong. He was very good at harpooning.

to Conseil. "We are going to look very silly to the scientists at home."

Conseil started to answer. But just then there was a yell. It was Ned Land.

"**Ahoy!** There it is at last!"

The whole crew ran toward Ned. He had made no mistake. It was the sea unicorn all right. The monster glowed in the dark. It was huge. And it was coming straight at us!

"Let's get away from it," said Commander Farragut. "We won't **stand a chance against** this animal if we fight at night. We'll wait until morning."

No one thought about sleeping. We could hear the giant animal breathing. We could see it glowing under the water.

Early in the morning Commander Farragut gave the order to attack. What a chase it was! The *Abraham Lincoln* charged forward. We were moving at a speed of fifteen **knots**. Then seventeen. Then eighteen knots! But the monster always stayed in front of us.

....

Ahoy! Look over there!
stand a chance against be able to beat
knots sea miles per hour

We got up to nineteen knots. Then the animal started zipping in rings around our ship! An angry cry **broke** from the crew.

"**Man** the guns!" cried Farragut. But our cannonballs bounced right off the hide of the giant animal!

....

broke came
Man Fire

The *Abraham Lincoln* **put up a hard fight**. But when night returned, we had gained nothing. We stopped the chase. The sea was dark.

At 10:50 p.m. the monster's bright light came on again. This was our chance. Farragut knew that the animal would have to rest after our fight. He gave orders to **creep up on** the animal while it was sleeping. Ned Land stood ready. He carried his harpoon.

We sailed closer . . . closer. . . . We were only a few feet away from the light! I saw Ned Land's arm go up. His harpoon shot out. I heard a loud ringing sound.

The animal's light went out. The monster then shot two huge jets of water at our ship. There was a **heavy jolt**. I was thrown into the sea!

....

put up a hard fight fought hard
creep up on move quietly toward
heavy jolt crash

BEFORE YOU MOVE ON...

1. **Comparisons** Reread page 8. How did the men feel at the start of the search? How did they feel four months later?

2. **Foreshadowing** Reread page 12. The Thing had lights and a hard body. Could it be something other than an animal?

LOOK AHEAD Read pages 13–17 to meet Captain Nemo.

Professor Aronnax, Ned Land, and Conseil land on the sea monster. But it is not a monster at all.

Chapter 3

When I **came to**, I was lying on something cold and hard. Conseil was there. And so was Ned Land.

"Look, Professor," said Ned. "Here is why my harpoon could not hurt this animal. Your sea unicorn is made of steel!"

I jumped up. We were on the back of the monster! But the "animal" was a machine! A ship that could sail *under* the sea!

"What happened?" I asked.

"We ran into this submarine," said Conseil. "The *Abraham Lincoln* got away. But we three were **washed overboard** by this thing's jets."

We heard a click. A **hatch** opened. Eight big, strong men appeared. Without making a sound, they dragged us down inside the ship. It all

....

came to woke up
washed overboard thrown into the ocean
hatch small door

happened **faster than lightning**.

The men locked us inside a small room. Hours later a door opened. Two men stepped inside. I could tell that one of them was the captain. He acted as though he was used to **giving orders**. He was a tall man with black hair and black eyes. His head sat nobly on his wide neck and shoulders. He had a proud look in his eye.

The captain waved his hand. Some men appeared. They brought dry clothes for us. The clothes were made of a beautiful, soft cloth. Other men brought in a table and some chairs. Then a waiter came in carrying our dinner.

We ate greedily. Our food was served on silver dishes. Each dish was marked with a large letter N. Most of the food was strange to us.

We were **filled with wonder**. Where were we? What ship was this? Who was this captain? What country did he come from?

The captain and his men spoke to each other in a strange language. I had never heard it before. The men did not seem to understand anything we said to them.

....

faster than lightning really quickly
giving orders telling people what to do
filled with wonder very curious about everything

But then, to my surprise, the captain spoke to me in French.

"Well!" he said. "What shall I do with you three? After all, I have the right to treat you as enemies. You were on a ship that attacked mine. If I wanted to, I could put you back up on the deck. I would give the order to dive and let you three drown. Wouldn't I have the right to do that?"

"That is not the right of a **civilized man**!" I cried.

"I am not a civilized man!" the captain replied. "I have left the company of other people. I will live forever under the sea! I will make my own laws!"

There was an angry flash in his eyes. I felt sure that something terrible had happened in his past.

"But I will let you live," the captain went on, "if you promise me one thing. There are certain things you must not see. So every now and then you must let yourselves be **shut away** again. The rest of the time you may have your freedom."

"Then you'll take us back to Europe?" I asked.

"No!" he cried. "You will never leave this ship!"

"Then you are not giving us freedom," I said. "You are just giving us the choice between life and

....

civilized man man who lives with other people
shut away prisoners

16

death. We will choose life in that case."

The captain bowed. "You will not find it so bad, Professor Aronnax", he said. "That's right—I know who you are! I even have your book in my library. It's pretty good, **as far as it goes**. But now, Professor, **a new world will open for you**. We are going to take an underwater trip to every sea of the globe. Thanks to me, you will see what no scientist has seen before."

I must say **his words touched my weak spot**. What scientist would not feel that way? Here was my chance! After such a trip, what a book I could write! My name would be famous all over the world!

"What shall we call you, sir?" I asked.

"To you," he replied, "I am just Captain Nemo. My ship is the *Nautilus*. May I show you around?"

We were bursting to see everything. So of course we followed Captain Nemo. The truth was more amazing than we could have dreamed.

....

as far as it goes but there is a lot that you don't know

a new world will open for you you will see new things here

his words touched my weak spot what he said interested me

BEFORE YOU MOVE ON...

1. **Conclusions** Reread page 16. How can you tell something bad might have happened in the captain's past?

2. **Setting** How was being on the *Nautilus* good for the professor? How was it bad?

LOOK AHEAD Read pages 18–22 to learn more about the *Nautilus*.

The front part of the *Nautilus* was where Captain
Nemo lived. The first room from the center of the
ship was the dining room.

In front of the dining room was a large library.
I gasped with joy when I saw it. There were more
than twelve thousand books. Hundreds of the books

were about ocean science. It was an underwater university!

The next room was the Grand Salon. Captain Nemo used this big room as a living room. There were some dials and meters on one wall. These instruments helped him watch over the ship at all times.

The salon was also a museum. Lovely old pictures hung on the walls. Against one wall there was an organ. On top of it were piles of music by the world's finest **composers**. Best of all, the museum was full of the sea's treasures. There were glass boxes full of beautiful shells, stones, and jewels.

Beyond the salon was my cabin. It was a large, comfortable room. Captain Nemo's bedroom was next door. It was also a large room. But it was much plainer than mine. More dials and meters hung on the walls.

We walked down a long hall, back to the center of the *Nautilus*. Right in the middle of the ship there was a kind of open **well**. I noticed a ladder going up from this well.

"That ladder goes up to a little room," Captain Nemo explained. "Inside there is a dinghy. The little boat has oars and a sail. I use the dinghy when I want to row on the surface of the ocean. I just shoot that whole room up to the top. Then I open the hatch and I'm on the water."

....

composers music writers
well tunnel in the ceiling

Just behind the center stairwell was a small cabin. Conseil and Ned Land were to share it. Next came the kitchen, baths, water tanks, and storerooms. After that were rooms for the crew. At the tail of the ship was the engine room.

The *Nautilus* worked entirely on electricity. It was far stronger than any electricity we knew about on land. Electric power ran the ship's engine. It gave us light. It cooked our food and warmed our rooms. It heated our water and gave us clean air.

The *Nautilus* breathed like a whale. It rose to the top for air. But it could also store air in its tanks. The ship could stay under the water for three days at a time.

Captain Nemo told us how he had built the ship. He had made each part in a different country. He had put the parts together on an island in the middle of the Pacific Ocean.

"You must be very rich!" I exclaimed.

"**Fabulously** rich, Professor," he replied. We stared at him in wonder.

....

Fabulously Very

When we finished looking over the ship, Nemo took us up on deck. He checked our **position**. We were three hundred miles or so off the coast of Japan. It was exactly noon, November 7, 1867. So began our adventure under the sea.

....

position location in the ocean

BEFORE YOU MOVE ON...

1. **Conclusions** The *Nautilus* was huge. What evidence supports this?

2. **Setting** Think about everything on the *Nautilus*. What does the ship tell you about Captain Nemo?

LOOK AHEAD Read pages 23–26. How do the prisoners feel?

The professor sees amazing fish in the ocean.
The Nautilus *is beautiful, but it is also a prison.*

Chapter 4

Conseil, Ned, and I went back down to the salon. A few minutes later we felt the ship dive.

We were amazed and afraid. And we **could talk about nothing but** the captain. **What was his story?** Why did he live on the *Nautilus*? And his name, Nemo. That word was Latin for "no one." *Who was this man?*

"Look!" cried Conseil. "The walls are moving!"

Sure enough, two walls were sliding open. One on each side of the big room. Behind the walls were sheets of glass. The *Nautilus* turned on its light. We could see out into the ocean for more than a mile on either side!

....

could talk about nothing but only talked about
What was his story? What had happened in his past?
Sure enough Yes

"Look at the fish!" said Conseil. "It's like a giant aquarium."

"No," I replied. "We are the ones who are **shut in**. Those fish are as free as the birds of the air."

We watched for almost two hours. **An army** of ocean animals swam with the *Nautilus*. It was wonderful! All kinds of fish appeared **before my dazzled** eyes. What a book this was going to make!

Suddenly the lights outside the salon went off. The walls slid closed. The show was over.

....

shut in trapped
An army A lot
before my dazzled in front of my amazed

BEFORE YOU MOVE ON...

1. **Paraphrase** Tell in your own words what the professor meant when he said: "We were amazed and afraid."

2. **Inference** *Nemo* means "no one" in Latin. Why do you think Nemo called himself this?

LOOK AHEAD Read pages 27–34 to find out how the prisoners get on land.

The Nautilus *sails for along time, but then suddenly stops. The prisoners make a plan to go to an island.*

Chapter 5

During the weeks that followed, Captain Nemo **kept to himself**. Every day his **first mate** came into the salon. He marked our location on the map. So I knew where we were going.

Whenever the ship rose for air, I went up on deck. It helped to get out under an open sky. At times men from the crew would be there. They spoke to each other in their strange language.

Our general direction was southeast. On November 27 we passed the Hawaiian Islands. On December 4 we reached the Marquesas Islands. We spotted the Tuamotu Islands on December 11.

We crossed the Tropic of Capricorn. Then we changed our direction. Now we were sailing northwest. We followed the great island chain across the South Pacific.

....

kept to himself preferred to be alone
first mate assistant

We reached the coast of Papua, New Guinea, on January 4. Here Captain Nemo told me that we were heading for the Indian Ocean. We would go through the Torres Strait.

The news **pleased Ned Land**. The Torres Strait separates Papua from Australia. We would be close to European waters. Ned thought we might be able to escape.

I was not so sure. I had heard that the Torres Strait was a very dangerous place. Many ships had been lost in its wild seas. Would the *Nautilus* **make** the trip?

At first we slipped through the rough waves easily. But then there was a jolt. We had hit something!

We were sitting on a **coral reef**. About two miles away we could see a small island. The *Nautilus* had not been hurt. All we had to do was wait for the tide to rise. Then we would float off the reef.

The tides in the Pacific are very low. Right then the tide was too low to lift the ship. We would have

....

pleased Ned Land made Ned Land happy
make survive
coral reef ridge made of coral

to wait until the next full moon. That was five days away.

Ned had an idea. "Let's ask Captain Nemo if we can visit that island over there," he said. "We could hunt for meat. I'm tired of seaweed and fish."

To my surprise, Captain Nemo said we could go ashore. Being on land again was exciting. Two months had passed since we had **set foot on firm ground**.

The island was covered with giant trees. Some were up to two hundred feet tall. We **set off** into the jungle to hunt. Ned shot a wild pig and some kangaroos. Conseil and I **brought down** some big birds.

By six that evening we were back on the beach. We ate a big dinner around a roaring fire. The air was filled with delightful smells.

"What do you say we don't go back to the *Nautilus* tonight?" Conseil asked.

"Let's not go back at all!" said Ned.

Just then a stone landed in front of us! We jumped to our feet and raised our guns. About a

---

set foot on firm ground been on land
set off went
brought down killed

hundred yards to our right stood more than fifty natives. They were armed with slings and bows and arrows.

"Men with weapons!" I yelled. "Back to the boat!"

Ned would not go without his meat. He loaded the kangaroos, the pigs, and the birds onto his shoulders. Then he ran. We were back in the dinghy **in minutes flat**. We rowed as fast as we could. Soon we were beyond the reach of the arrows.

Before long we were safely back on the *Nautilus*. I ran to find Captain Nemo. He was in the salon, playing the organ.

"Captain!" I yelled. He did not even hear me. "Captain Nemo! There are men out there!"

He turned and smiled. "Why, what else did you expect to find on land, Professor?" he asked.

"But there are over a hundred of them! And they are going to attack us!" I cried. "They have weapons."

Nemo ran his fingers lightly over the organ keys. "Even if all the natives in Papua attacked, we would be safe," he said. He went back to his music.

The night passed. I went up on deck early the next morning. By now there were over five hundred

---

in minutes flat very quickly

natives on the beach. Some of them had brought their **canoes** out to the coral reefs. They were standing only a few yards away from me.

More canoes left the shore. Soon it was clear that the natives were going to surround the ship. I went **below**. Captain Nemo closed the hatches.

The tide was due to lift us off the reef at 2:40 p.m. on January 9. At 2:00 I could feel the water starting to lift the ship. Soon we would have to open the

....

canoes boats
below back into the submarine

33

hatches to **change the air**. The moment we did that, the armed men would enter the ship!

At 2:35 Captain Nemo gave the order. The hatches were opened. I stood ready with my gun.

Sure enough, I saw twenty or thirty of those faces looking in. One of the men began to climb down.

He was thrown back as if by an unseen force! He cried out in pain and dived into the water.

At last I understood. **The ship was electrified!** All Captain Nemo had to do was flip a switch. And no one could even touch the *Nautilus*!

At that moment the tide rose. The *Nautilus* floated off her coral bed. We started our engines. Then we sailed smoothly on through the Torres Strait. We were **safe and sound**.

....

change the air get fresh air

The ship was electrified! The ship was protected by electricity!

safe and sound completely safe

BEFORE YOU MOVE ON...

1. **Cause and Effect** Reread pages 28–29. Why did the prisoners have time to go to the island?

2. **Cause and Effect** Reread page 31. Why were the prisoners afraid of the men on the land?

LOOK AHEAD Read pages 35–39 to find out who dies.

Captain Nemo keeps secrets from the prisoners.
They are locked in a room when something
terrible happens.

Chapter 6

It was January 18. We were now in the middle
of the Indian Ocean. I went up on deck for my
morning air.

As usual, I saw one of the sailors appear. He
looked out over the sea. This time what he saw
scared him. He hurried below.

A minute later Captain Nemo came up on deck.
He took the **spyglass** from the sailor. He looked
hard at the water. Then he and the sailor began to
talk in excited voices.

I thought I would see what **all the fuss was**
about. I lifted my own spyglass to my eye. Captain
Nemo snatched it from my hand.

"You must not see that!" he cried. "I'm sorry,
Professor. But now I am going to ask you to keep

....

spyglass telescope

all the fuss was they were concerned

the promise you made. You must let me make you a prisoner again."

I had no choice, so I went below. Four men were waiting for me. They took me to a small room. Ned and Conseil were there, too.

Before long they brought us a meal. Since there was nothing else to do, we ate it. Then we each sat down in a corner.

To my surprise Ned Land fell right to sleep. Then Conseil also **dropped into a deep slumber**. I yawned. My eyes closed. I heard the hatches closing and felt the ship starting to dive. I thought, "Nemo drugged our food!" And then I **passed out**.

I woke up in my own room hours later. I found that I was free once again. So I wandered up to the deck. Ned and Conseil were already there. The sea was calm and the sun was shining. There was no sign that anything strange had happened.

That afternoon I was in the salon, working on my notes. Captain Nemo came in. He looked sad and tired.

"Are you by some chance a doctor, Professor Aronnax?" he asked.

....

dropped into a deep slumber fell asleep
passed out fell asleep

"Why, yes," I replied. **"I was in medicine before I joined the museum."**

"Then would you please have a look at one of my men?"

He led me to a cabin near the back of the ship. There lay a man of about forty. Bandages covered his eyes and head. I undid them and looked. The poor man's head had been smashed.

I felt the man's pulse. It was **fading fast**. His hands were already starting to get cold.

"There is nothing I can do," I told Nemo. "This man will die within two hours."

Nemo's eyes filled with tears. "Please leave me alone with him then, Professor," he said.

That night I heard some men singing. The song sounded like a **hymn**.

The next morning Nemo invited us to go on a walk underwater. We put on diving suits and carried our own air in tanks. About a dozen men from the crew came along. We walked for about two hours, down to nine hundred feet. Then we entered a cave made of coral.

....

"I was in medicine before I joined the museum." "I was a doctor before I became a scientist."

fading fast losing strength

hymn religious song

The men stopped. I saw that four of them were carrying a long bundle across their shoulders.

We were at a funeral! They were burying the man who had died during the night. I watched **in shock** as the sailors dug the grave. In the shadows I could see the **mounds** of other graves. I also saw a huge cross of coral.

The men lowered the body into its **last resting place**. Then, with sad hearts, we made our way back to the *Nautilus*.

....

in shock feeling very surprised
mounds evidence
last resting place grave

BEFORE YOU MOVE ON...

1. **Summarize** One of the men on the ship died. Why didn't the prisoners know what caused his death?

2. **Conclusions** More people from the *Nautilus* have died in the past. How do you know?

LOOK AHEAD Read pages 40–45. Is Captain Nemo a good person?

Captain Nemo takes the prisoners to look for pearls.
They meet a diver and are attacked by a shark.

Chapter 7

The death of the sailor changed my feelings about Captain Nemo. Now I not only admired him—I was also afraid of him. I knew that sometimes he attacked other ships. While we slept, the *Nautilus* had been in some kind of fight. I was sure of it.

Captain Nemo had changed, too. He sometimes looked sad or angry. Often he would stay in his cabin. I would not see him for days at a time.

We kept sailing west, through the Indian Ocean. On January 28 we saw the island of Ceylon. Ceylon is famous for its pearls. Captain Nemo told me about the men who fished for pearls.

"They dive by holding on to heavy stones," he said. "The stones are tied to boats by long ropes.

"A diver can stay **down** for only half a minute at a time. Then he goes up to the boat and pulls the

---

down underwater

stone up after him. He gets paid less than a penny for every pearl he finds."

"That's terrible!" I cried. "A penny a pearl for these poor people. While their masters get rich!"

The next morning Captain Nemo took us to hunt for pearls. We went in the dinghy. At about six in the morning we **dropped anchor**. We put on our diving suits.

Once more Nemo led us along the ocean floor. He followed paths that only he knew. He led us to a deep cave. In it lay the biggest oyster I had ever seen. Inside the oyster was a pearl as big as a coconut.

I gasped. Why, this pearl alone was worth **ten million francs**. I wondered how many other treasures Nemo had, hidden in the ocean.

We left the cave and walked among **ocean beds of** oysters. Suddenly Nemo stopped. He signaled for us to hide behind some rocks. Then he pointed.

A shadow appeared a few feet away. It dropped to the ocean floor. I thought of sharks. But it was only one of those poor Indian divers. He was

....

dropped anchor held the boat in place with an anchor
ten million francs a lot of French money
ocean beds of areas filled with

holding on to a stone. The stone was tied to the end of a long rope.

When the diver hit the bottom, he quickly filled a small bag with oysters. Then he swam back to the top.

We watched as the diver went up and down.
He could pick up only about ten oysters with
each dive.

Suddenly the man looked up in terror. A huge
shark was moving toward him! Its wide jaws were
open. There was fire in its eyes!

The diver jumped to one side. The shark's bite missed him. But the shark's tail knocked him **flat**.

Captain Nemo moved quickly. He tore into the shark with his knife. A terrible fight followed. The water turned red with blood. The captain was knocked to the ground. The shark opened its jaws. It looked like **it was all over for Nemo**!

But Ned Land acted as fast as lightning. His harpoon hit the shark's heart. In seconds the shark was dead.

----

flat down

it was all over for Nemo Nemo would die

The diver was caught in his rope. We cut him loose and took him up to his boat. Nemo **brought him back to life**. The Indian opened his eyes.

What did the diver think when he saw our diving helmets bending over him? Or when Captain Nemo handed him a whole bag of pearls? Or when we returned to the sea? He must surely have thought we were gods.

....

brought him back to life woke him up

BEFORE YOU MOVE ON...

1. **Character** Captain Nemo attacked the shark to save the pearl diver. What does this tell you about him?

2. **Character's Point of View** Reread page 45. Why might the diver think that Captain Nemo and the others were gods?

LOOK AHEAD Read pages 46–51 to find out why Ned is excited.

Near land, the three men hope to escape again. Captain Nemo takes the Nautilus *through a secret passage. The professor sees some of his treasure.*

Chapter 8

We left Ceylon and headed across the Arabian Sea. We crossed the Gulf of Oman, then turned southeast. We followed the shores of Arabia.

As we sailed Ned's excitement grew. We were now near civilization. We could even see the domes and towers of towns. Sometimes we saw French, Dutch, and English ships. They were on their way from Egypt to India and Australia.

Ned had an escape plan all worked out. We would wait for the right night. We would take the dinghy up to the surface. Then we would row to freedom. Now that land was so near, Ned watched for a chance to go.

On February 7 Nemo ordered the *Nautilus* to enter the Red Sea. We headed toward Egypt. We were getting nearer to Europe every minute!

But no chance to get away came. Most of the

time we stayed too far underwater to use the dinghy. We came up for air only when there were no ships in sight.

One day I asked Captain Nemo where we were going.

"Why, to Europe," he answered. "The day after tomorrow we will be in the Mediterranean Sea."

I could not believe **my ears**. A strip of land separated the Red Sea from the Mediterranean. But Captain Nemo had found a way through.

"It is a secret underground passage," he explained. "I call it the Arabian Tunnel."

We reached the northern tip of the Red Sea. Then we dived down, down, down. At last a wide, deep hole opened before us. The *Nautilus* moved right into it.

A loud rushing noise hit the ship. It was the water of the Red Sea moving toward the Mediterranean. The *Nautilus* was **swept along**.

In twenty minutes we had passed through the tunnel. We were in European waters!

But the *Nautilus* stayed in deep waters far from shore. No chance for escape came. I felt very sad.

....

my ears what I heard
swept along moving with the water

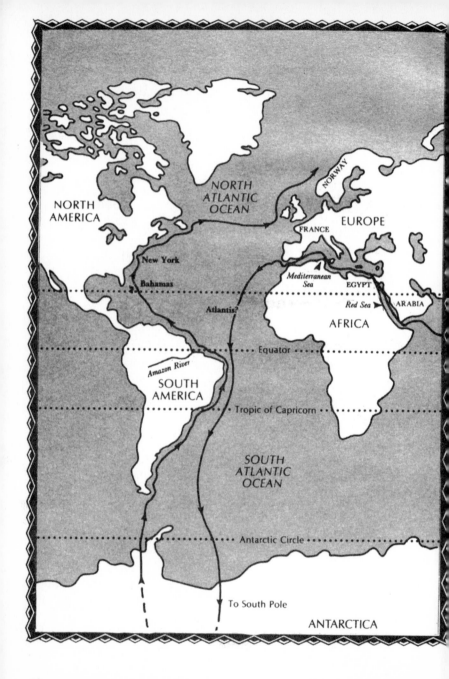

NORTH
ATLANTIC
OCEAN

NORTH
AMERICA

NORWAY

EUROPE

FRANCE

New York

Bahamas

*Mediterranean
Sea*

EGYPT

Atlantis?

Red Sea

ARABIA

AFRICA

Equator

Amazon River

SOUTH
AMERICA

Tropic of Capricorn

SOUTH
ATLANTIC
OCEAN

Antarctic Circle

To South Pole

ANTARCTICA

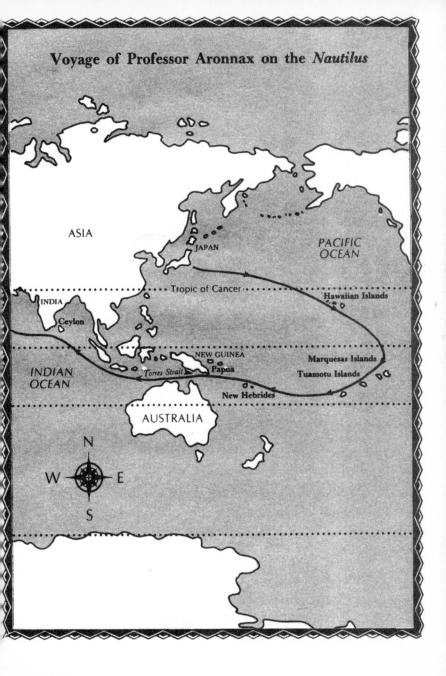

Voyage of Professor Aronnax on the *Nautilus*

ASIA

PACIFIC OCEAN

JAPAN

Tropic of Cancer

INDIA

Hawaiian Islands

Ceylon

NEW GUINEA

Marquesas Islands

INDIAN OCEAN

Torres Strait

Papua

Tuamotu Islands

New Hebrides

AUSTRALIA

N

W E

S

These very waters washed the free shores of France. But we were prisoners.

Now we were heading toward the island of Crete. I remembered that the people of Crete were at war. They were fighting for their freedom from the Turkish **emperor**.

We dropped anchor off the coast of Crete on the night of February 14. I spent that night in the salon with Captain Nemo. He had the side walls open. He walked back and forth. I could see that he was worried.

A diver appeared in the water outside. Nemo waved to him. "That's Nicholas, the Fish," Nemo said.

The captain unlocked a cabinet that stood along one wall. The cabinet was full of gold! I watched in amazement. Nemo filled a small **chest** with gold bars. Then he called two sailors to carry the chest away.

The next day it was clear that our business in

These very waters washed the free shores of France. We were so close to France.

emperor ruler

chest box

Europe was done. Nemo sailed west **at top speed**.
Late in the afternoon of February 18 we passed
through the Strait of Gibraltar. We were now in the
Atlantic Ocean.

....

at top speed quickly

BEFORE YOU MOVE ON...

1. **Details** Ned was excited because he thought
   they could escape. What was Ned's plan?

2. **Viewing** Look at the map on pages 48–49.
   How does it help you understand the story
   better?

LOOK AHEAD Read to page 54 to learn
more about the mysterious gold.

The Nautilus *stops to pick something up. Professor Aronnax learns more about Captain Nemo and where his treasure comes from.*

Chapter 9

The next day we tried to escape. We knew it might be our last chance for a while. We were only a few miles from Spain. Who could tell where we would be tomorrow?

We went over our plans. We were to meet at the center stairwell at nine o'clock. At exactly nine I heard a terrifying sound. Silence! The ship's engine had stopped! The only sound was my heart beating. The *Nautilus* was resting on the bottom of the ocean.

Captain Nemo came into the library. He did not seem to notice that I had on my outdoor clothes. "Hello, Professor," he said in a friendly voice. "Do you know the history of Spain?"

I was too scared to answer. Captain Nemo began to tell me a long story. It was all about the wreck of some French treasure ships. Then he led me into the salon and opened the side walls. At last I understood.

We were resting on a **clean stretch** of sand. I could see the French treasure ships out in the water. Sailors from the *Nautilus* were hard at work. They were emptying the chests from the ships.

---

clean stretch long area

So this was how Nemo got his money!

"Why, you are stealing this treasure!" I exclaimed.

That made Captain Nemo angry. "Do you think I take it just for myself?" he asked. "There are people in this world who are poor and sick. There are people who are fighting for freedom. I take the treasure for *them*."

So he had a heart after all! I looked at Captain Nemo **with new eyes**. For now I understood why we had visited the Mediterranean Sea. Captain Nemo had helped the freedom fighters on Crete. He had taken them a chest of gold.

....

So he had a heart after all! I realized Captain Nemo was actually a nice person!

with new eyes differently

BEFORE YOU MOVE ON...

1. **Character's Motive** What did Captain Nemo do with the gold bars from the cabinet? Why?

2. **Cause and Effect** What made the professor feel differently about Nemo?

LOOK AHEAD Read pages 55–58. Is the professor afraid of Captain Nemo?

The prisoners are not able to escape. But the professor has a magical journey.

Chapter 10

We had lost our chance to escape. That much was clear. We were now sailing southwest, away from Europe. I felt **as if a weight had been taken from my mind**. I went back to studying ocean life.

As often as I could, I opened the side walls. How I loved to see the fish swimming free! I saw sharks of all kinds. Giant swordfish and marlins. Even porpoises. A **school** of them swam with us for several days.

One night Captain Nemo asked me to go on another walk underwater. This time we went alone.

The *Nautilus* was resting at the foot of an underwater mountain. Nemo and I climbed to the top of this peak. It took us two hard hours.

....

as if a weight had been taken from my mind much less worried

school group

I could not believe what I saw when we
got to the top! We were looking down on a large,
flat plain. A volcano burned in the distance. Lava
poured from the volcano. The red-hot rocks lit up
an entire city.

For it was a city I saw there. I could see towers,
palaces, houses, stores. **All were lying in ruin.**

....

All were lying in ruin. All of them had been destroyed.

Beyond the city I could see what was left of a large wall.

Captain Nemo picked up a soft rock. With it he wrote on a piece of flat black stone:

ATLANTIS

Atlantis! The city of magic described by **Plato** and others long ago!

Plato said that Atlantis had once been the center of a mighty civilization. But then there was a terrible earthquake. Atlantis disappeared under the waves.

And now here I stood. I was looking at the ruins of that **legendary** city. Would there be no end to the wonders Captain Nemo would show me?

....

Plato   a famous man from Ancient Greece
legendary   famous

BEFORE YOU MOVE ON...

1. **Character's Point of View** How did Professor Aronnax feel about Captain Nemo? How do you know?

2. **Cause and Effect** Why was the professor surprised to see Atlantis?

LOOK AHEAD Read pages 59–68. Why does Nemo need to hurry?

The Nautilus *goes to the South Pole. The water freezes around the submarine.*

Chapter 11

Now the *Nautilus* headed straight south. We were going pretty fast. It looked like Nemo was planning to sail around the tip of South America. I figured we would return to the Pacific Ocean from there.

But instead we kept sailing south. The *Nautilus* stayed on the surface. The sea grew colder and colder. Chunks of ice began to appear. The farther south we sailed, the bigger the ice chunks became. In time the sea became no more than a river between **iceberg mountains**.

On March 16 we crossed the Antarctic Circle. I guessed that Captain Nemo planned to go all the way to the South Pole. No one had ever done that before. It turned out that I was right.

Captain Nemo **let me in on** his daring idea. The sea was frozen over now. But far down below the

....

iceberg mountains giant chunks of floating ice
let me in on told me about

ice shelf, the ocean still flowed. We would travel under the ice to the South Pole.

We filled our tanks with as much air as they would hold. At four in the afternoon on March 18 we dived. The ship went down twenty-five hundred feet before it found water that was free of ice. But after that we moved easily. I went to my room to get some rest.

The next morning we came out from under the ice shelf. I rushed up on deck for fresh air. There was an open sea around us.

"The South Pole should be over there," said Captain Nemo. He pointed to a mountain in the distance. We sailed toward the shore.

Now a new problem arose. Captain Nemo wanted to make sure he had reached the exact South Pole. He needed the sun to measure exactly where he was. But at the South Pole the sun shines day and night for six months of the year. For the other six months the sky is dark. The **changeovers** take place on the first day of spring and the first day of fall. The next day was March 21. Fall in this

....

ice shelf layer of ice
changeovers changes

part of the world. The long polar night would begin.

March 21 **dawned** clear and bright. Captain Nemo and I went ashore. We made our way across the rocks and up the side of the mountain. Nemo wanted to do his measuring from the top.

We were at the peak in two hours. It was now nearly noon. Captain Nemo put his spyglass to his eye. He watched the sun sinking. I kept my eye on our small watch. **My heart pounded.** The sun disappeared exactly at twelve. We were at the South Pole!

Captain Nemo took out a black flag. On it was a large letter N. "On this day, March 21, 1868, I claim the South Pole!" he cried. "In the name of—Captain Nemo!"

The next morning the *Nautilus* got ready to leave. We had to move fast. Winter was **setting in by the minute**. Already the open sea was starting to freeze.

That night we were once more under the ice

....

dawned started
My heart pounded. I was very excited.
setting in by the minute coming quickly

shelf. We headed north. I was **tired out by** my trip ashore. I fell asleep early.

A jolt woke me in the middle of the night. I was tumbled out of my bed into the middle of the floor. We had stopped! And the whole ship was turned on its side!

....

tired out by very tired because of

I pulled myself along the walls. I reached the salon. Ned and Conseil had already **made it** there. "We've hit an iceberg!" Ned cried. "It's all over for us now!"

Captain Nemo came in. "Don't worry," he told us. "An iceberg *did* hit us. We are one thousand

---

made it arrived

eighty feet under the water. And the ship is lying on its side. But we will soon be all right again. All we have to do is empty the air tanks and water tanks on one side."

Nemo was right. Ten minutes later we felt the ship moving under us. Soon we were floating again.

"A close escape!" Conseil cried.

"If we *have* escaped," said Ned Land.

At that moment the side walls opened. I was **gripped with fear**. But I had never seen anything more beautiful.

The *Nautilus* was inside a tunnel of ice. The light was so bright that we had to cover our eyes. The ice walls around us sparkled like jewels.

The lights and colors flashed faster. The *Nautilus* was speeding up. Faster and faster we sailed through that tunnel of white light.

There was another jolt! Our tunnel had ended. We had hit a solid wall of ice!

For a few minutes the ship sailed backward. But the other end of the ice tunnel was now frozen, too. We were trapped!

Again Captain Nemo stayed calm. He tested all the walls of our ice prison. "The thinnest wall is

....

gripped with fear very afraid

underneath us," he said. "We will start right away to dig our way down."

We set off in our diving suits and began to dig. We were making a big ditch in the ice. We took turns working all day. But we could see that it was **no use**. Our ditch was freezing over as fast as we could dig it.

As usual, Captain Nemo had an idea that saved **the day**. In the kitchen were big machines. These changed sea water into drinking water. Nemo ordered his crew to fill the machines with water. Then he turned the electricity up high.

The water got boiling hot. Then it was pumped back out into the sea. We pumped icy water in and boiling water out for three hours. It began to work! The water temperature slowly started to rise. The ice was no longer freezing back over!

We went back to digging with new energy. But the work grew harder and harder. We were running out of air. Soon there was almost no air left on the ship. It all had to be saved for the men who were digging.

Now only a few feet of ice were left. It was time

....

no use not helping
the day us

to use the *Nautilus* itself as a weapon. Everyone got back on board. Nemo moved the submarine right over our ditch. Then he ordered all the tanks to be filled with water.

The *Nautilus* dropped straight down like a stone. There was a sound like tearing paper. We crashed through the ice!

But we weren't out of danger yet. We were still under the ice shelf. And our air was almost gone.

Would we make it out in time? I didn't think so. **My face was turning blue.** I could no longer see or hear. I thought I was going to die.

Suddenly the *Nautilus* stopped. We changed position. Now we were pointing up. We shot forward. Our long steel nose **rammed** the ice ceiling. There was a boom. A jolt. Another charge! Another jolt! We were breaking the ice like a giant **ice pick**!

The ice cracked! The crack got wider! With a final crash the ship broke out of its ice prison. Fresh air!

....

My face was turning blue. I couldn't breathe.

rammed hit

ice pick ice-breaking tool

BEFORE YOU MOVE ON...

1. **Cause and Effect** Explain why Captain Nemo had to be at the South Pole by March 21.

2. **Plot** The *Nautilus* got stuck in an ice tunnel. How did Nemo solve the problem?

LOOK AHEAD Read pages 69–74 to learn where the *Nautilus* goes next.

Professor Aronnax is enjoying the trip. Then the ship and crew must fight a real sea monster.

Chapter 12

We sailed north as fast as our **propellers would carry us**. We reached the tip of South America on March 31. By April 11 we were at **the mouth of** the Amazon River. The *Nautilus* stayed there for two days. The men fished and stored up food.

Ned, Conseil, and I spent most of those two days up on deck. We took in all the sun, warmth, and fresh air we could get.

We were near the Bahamas by April 20. Many ships crossed this part of the ocean. So Captain Nemo kept the *Nautilus* underwater.

How amazing life was down there! I never got tired of opening the side walls and looking out at the fish.

The fish in these waters were among the most beautiful in the world. They were colored as

....

propellers would carry us ship could go
the mouth of an entrance to

brightly as jewels. They swam among the giant seaweed that grew from the ocean floor.

"Look at the size of those plants," I said to Conseil. "They could be a salad for some giant sea animal."

"I don't believe in giant sea animals," said Ned Land. "Remember your sea unicorn? It turned out to be a submarine."

"But there *are* giant animals in the ocean!" I said. "There's the giant squid, for example."

"Giant squid?" Ned laughed. "What does this monster look like?"

"Well," said Conseil, "it's about twenty feet long."

"That's right!" I said.

"And it has eight big arms that look like horrible snakes," Conseil went on.

"Exactly," I said.

"And its eyes are at the back of its head. And its mouth is like a parrot's beak. Only it is much, much bigger," said Conseil.

"Right again!" I was amazed at how many facts Conseil remembered. But then I turned around. I screamed. A giant squid was looking right at us! And I could see six or seven more squids behind it.

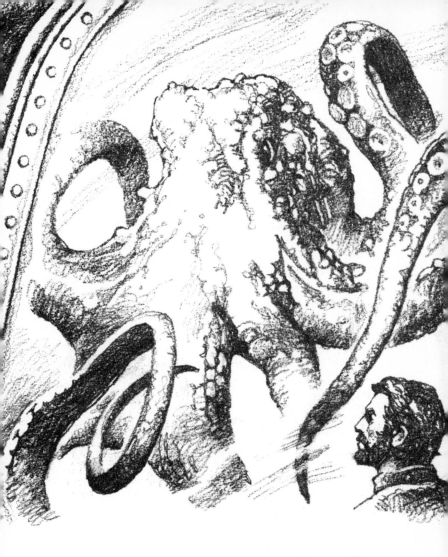

The monster came right up to the glass wall.
It looked at us with huge blue-green eyes. The giant
squid was over twenty-five feet long! Its huge arms

had suckers on them. The thing must have weighed fifty thousand pounds. And it looked very angry.

We soon found out what was making it mad. Captain Nemo came and told us. "One of those squids is caught on our propeller," he explained, "and our guns are useless against it. Squids' bodies are so soft that bullets go right through them. We'll have to cut the creature off."

"What you need is a good harpooner!" cried Ned. "Let me help!"

The *Nautilus* rose to the surface. The men armed themselves with harpoons and axes. They charged up the ladder. The first man unlocked the hatch.

The hatch flew open! It had been **yanked** up by one of the suckers on a giant squid's arm! Another huge arm slid down the ladder like a snake. Captain Nemo cut it off with one blow of his ax.

Another arm slithered down. This time it wrapped itself around a sailor's waist!

"Help! Help!" the man cried. But the squid pulled him out of the ship.

"A bloody battle followed. We **slashed away at** the squid from all sides. For a while it looked as if

....

yanked pulled

slashed away at tried to cut

we would save the man. We cut off seven of those terrible arms. But the eighth arm waved the sailor around like a feather.

Then the squid squirted us with thick black ink. When we could see again, the squid had disappeared.

We threw ourselves in fury against the rest of the squids. Over and over we slashed at those slimy arms. In fifteen minutes we had finished and won the battle.

But we had lost a man. After the fight Captain Nemo stood for a long time staring out into the sea. Tears ran down his face.

....

We threw ourselves in fury We fought hard

BEFORE YOU MOVE ON...

1. **Character's Point of View** Why did the professor enjoy the ocean near the Bahamas?

2. **Paraphrase** Reread page 72. Tell in your own words how the squid's arm got into the submarine.

LOOK AHEAD Read to page 80. Will Ned finally try to escape?

Professor Aronnax is ready to escape. But then, Captain Nemo attacks a passing ship.

Chapter 13

By now I had come around to Ned Land's point of view. We had to escape—soon.

On May 1 we reached the Bahamas. There we entered the Gulf Stream. This is a strong, warm **current**. It runs like a river around the North Atlantic. Then it sweeps up the North American coast and across to Europe.

I had great hopes for escaping once we were in this stream. We were following the American coast, going north. We were nearing New York.

But alas! A storm kept us far away from the shores of America. Another storm kept us from the ports of Canada. By May 25 we were once again in the middle of the Atlantic. On May 28 we were a hundred miles off the coast of Ireland.

....

current path of water
But alas! But no!

We were sailing southwest of England on June 1. The sea was calm and the sky was clear. Captain Nemo came up on deck. About eight miles to the east there was a big ship. The ship seemed to be coming our way.

Captain Nemo went back down the hatch. I followed him. Had he noticed the other ship? I could not tell. A few minutes later he gave the order to dive.

We came up again a few hours later. I heard a boom. I ran up to the deck to see what it was. Ned and Conseil were there.

"That ship's getting closer!" Ned cried. "We may have a chance to swim **for it**!"

A shell splashed in the water near us. "**Great heavens!**" I yelled. "It's a warship! And it's firing at us!"

Then **the truth hit me**. Of course! The *Abraham Lincoln* had gotten close to the sea unicorn. Commander Farragut had seen that it was a submarine. He had spread the news. By now all

....

for it to safety

Great heavens! Oh no!

the truth hit me I realized what was happening

the navies of the world were probably **after** Captain Nemo.

"It's got to be Farragut!" cried Ned. "I'm going to signal!" He waved his handkerchief. An iron fist struck him. Ned fell to the deck.

Captain Nemo had hit him! Nemo was terrifying to see. His face was white. His eyes were blacker than ever. He shook his fist at me.

"You and your friends get below!" he roared.

"You're not going to attack that ship!" I exclaimed.

Nemo clenched his teeth in hate. "I am going to sink it," he replied. "Now get below! Not another word from you!"

I did not sleep that night. The terrible day of June 2 dawned. The other ship drew very close. I could not tell what ship it was. The sound of gunfire was all around.

I heard the hatches close. The *Nautilus* dived. Then she pointed up again. She **gunned** her motors. Her speed picked up. With a sinking

---

after looking for
gunned increased the speed of

stomach I knew what Nemo was going to do. He was going to ram the warship!

Our steel nose tore through the warship as easily as a needle passes through cloth. I could **stand it** no longer! I rushed into the salon. There stood Captain Nemo. He had the side walls open. He was watching the other ship **go down**.

The warship sank slowly. The *Nautilus* followed

....

stand it sit still
go down sink

it down. The drowning crew climbed up the
warship's **masts** like ants. Then the ship **blew up**.
It and all its men were swallowed by the sea.

Captain Nemo turned away. He walked into
his room. I followed him. On the far wall I saw
a picture. I had never seen it before. It showed a
young woman with two small children.

Captain Nemo stood in front of this picture

....

masts poles
blew up exploded

for several minutes. Then he fell to his knees. He stretched out his arms toward the young woman. **He burst into deep sobs.**

....

He burst into deep sobs. He started crying.

BEFORE YOU MOVE ON...

1. **Cause and Effect** Why did Ned try to signal the ship?

2. **Inference** How did Nemo feel about the woman and the children in the picture? How can you tell?

LOOK AHEAD Read pages 81–85 to find out how Captain Nemo changes.

***The* Nautilus *sails without any direction.*
*Finally, the prisoners can escape!***

Chapter 14

From that day on my only thought was escape. I was afraid of Captain Nemo. I was scared of the hatred in his soul. What sadness **lay** in his past? I did not know. But I felt sure that he had loved the woman in the picture. I believed that she had something to do with the ship we had attacked. Perhaps she had been killed at sea. Perhaps Captain Nemo had sunk the ship in revenge. **Those drowning men would not leave my mind.** I had nightmares and couldn't sleep.

The *Nautilus* seemed to have lost its sense of direction. It sailed here and there around the North Atlantic. It never came up except for air. Neither Captain Nemo nor the first mate appeared. No one marked our location on the map. I had no idea

....

lay was

Those drowning men would not leave my mind. I couldn't stop thinking about the men who had drowned.

where we were. We wandered like that for more than two weeks.

Then early one morning Ned sneaked into my room.

"We are going to escape tonight," he whispered. "I sighted land this morning. I don't know what country it is. But we have to try to get there. We go at ten tonight."

Another long day **dragged on**. I collected my notes and hid them **on my body**. Once more I dressed in my warm clothes. I waited in my room.

Just before ten a terrifying sound came from the salon. Organ music! Captain Nemo was playing. And I had to pass by him to escape!

I crept across the hall and quietly opened the salon door. Nemo didn't see me. I dropped to my knees. I crawled slowly across the carpet.

Just as I reached the library door, Nemo stood up and walked right toward me. But he still didn't see me. He was sobbing and **murmuring** like a ghost.

....

dragged on passed slowly
on my body in my clothes
murmuring talking softly

"Enough!" he cried. "Enough!" Those were the last words I would hear him speak.

Moments later Ned Land, Conseil, and I were inside the dinghy. Ned reached for the switch that would shoot us to the surface.

Suddenly we heard excited voices inside the *Nautilus*. Had our escape been discovered? No! The sailors were shouting in fear. Over and over they were screaming one horrifying word: "**Whirlpool!**"

A whirlpool! The *Nautilus* was being sucked under! A huge roar blasted our ears. We were tossed about like a cork on the waves!

"Hold on!" yelled Ned. "Stay with the ship! We may **yet be saved**!"

Just then there was a loud crack. The dinghy was torn away from the ship. We shot up **like a stone out of a slingshot**. My head hit the side of the dinghy. Everything went black.

I don't know how we got out of the whirlpool. But when I awoke, I was lying in a fisherman's hut. That is where I am now. Ned Land and Conseil are here, too. We are on an island off the coast of Norway.

Whirlpool! Spinning circle of water!
yet be saved live
like a stone out of a slingshot quickly

We will be here for another two weeks. Until the next **steamer** comes through. Then we will head for France. I've spent the time here putting my notes together. What a book this is going to make!

What happened to the *Nautilus*? Did she escape the whirlpool? Is Captain Nemo still alive?

I don't know. I hope so. I hope Captain Nemo has found peace. I hope he will **turn his mind to** science and not war. Above all, I hope he is still sailing his beloved *Nautilus* beneath the sea.

....

steamer big ship
turn his mind to start caring about

BEFORE YOU MOVE ON...

1. **Comparisons** Captain Nemo changed after they sank the warship. How was he different?

2. **Inference** Reread pages 84–85. What do you think Professor Aronnax will do after his *Nautilus* journey?